Let's Read!

 Read the Page

Say It   Sound It   Spell It

Why is wh yellow?

Yellow highlights represent letter teams that make a single sound or words with irregular decoding patterns.

Look At Della Duck

Story by Rozanne Lanczak Williams
Illustrated by Yakovetic Productions

 Look at Della Duck.
See what she can do.

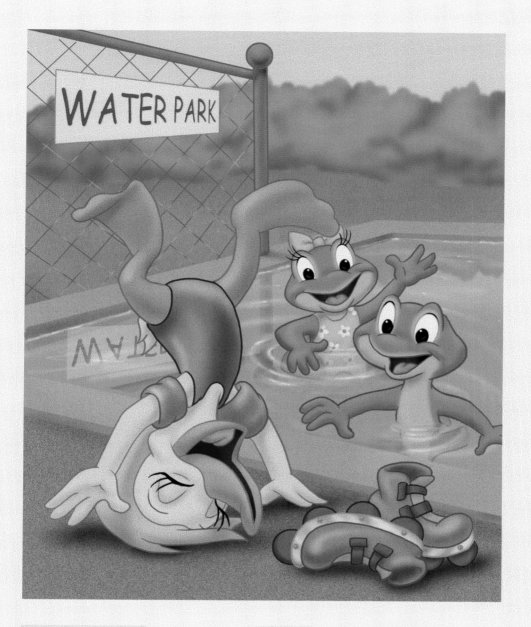

Della can do tricks
just for me and you.

 Della climbs up
to the tip, tip, top.

She can flip.
She can flop.

She can land with a plop!

Look at Della Duck.
She slides on her
tummy.

She slips off the slide. Leap thinks it's funny.

Look at Della Duck
as she steps over
the mud.

 She whirls and
she twirls.
Then she falls...

with a thud!

 Look at Della Duck.
See what she can do.
Della can do tricks
just for me and you!